Ladybird

Aladdin

Disney

One dark night, in a faraway land, a man named Jafar stood waiting in the desert. He was the Royal Vizier, the most trusted adviser to the Sultan of Agrabah, but he had a wicked heart and evil plans. A thief called Gazeem had promised to bring him something that would make Jafar the most powerful man in Agrabah.

At last, in the distance, Jafar saw a rider approaching. "He's coming, Iago," Jafar said to the parrot on his shoulder.

"Do you have it?" Jafar asked anxiously as Gazeem drew near.

Gazeem handed Jafar half of a sacred scarab medallion. Jafar fitted it to the half he already had – and the medallion instantly shone with a magical glow.

"At last," breathed Jafar, his heart pounding with excitement. "This medallion will open the Tiger-God's Cave of Wonders, where the greatest treasure of all is hidden – the magic lamp!"

"Awk! Magic lamp!" squawked Iago.

"Yes," said Jafar. "And the magic lamp will be *mine*, as soon as we find the one person the Tiger-God will allow into the cave. He must be someone common and ordinary, but with a pure heart – a Diamond in the Rough!"

Jafar soon learned who that Diamond in the Rough was. He was a poor, ragged street boy called Aladdin, whose home was a rooftop in Agrabah. Somehow, Jafar would have to capture Aladdin and trick him into getting the lamp for him.

Miles from the desert, Aladdin was about to share a crust of bread with Abu, his pet monkey.

"Some day, Abu," said Aladdin, looking out over the city, "things will be different. We'll live in a palace, like princes!"

For now, though, all Aladdin could do was dream.

In the palace of Agrabah, the Sultan's daughter, Jasmine, had just rejected another suitor.

The Sultan was exasperated. "You know the law," he said to Jasmine. "You must marry a prince before your next birthday – and that's only three days away!"

But Jasmine would not marry anyone she didn't love, not even a prince.

Jasmine was bored with palace life, and tired of having decisions made for her. She knew that there was only one way to avoid being forced into marriage – she had to run away.

Early the next morning, disguised in a long cloak, she secretly climbed over the palace wall and crept into the town.

In the marketplace, Aladdin watched the beautiful stranger wander from stall to stall. There was something special about her, something he couldn't explain. He just couldn't stop staring at her!

When a fruit seller accused Jasmine of trying to steal one of his apples, Aladdin rushed to her rescue. They ran through the marketplace and up to Aladdin's rooftop.

They had just caught their breath when Rasoul, one of Jafar's guards, suddenly loomed over them. "You're under arrest!" he said to Aladdin.

Jasmine stepped forward. "Release him, by order of the Princess," she commanded, throwing back her cloak.

"The *Princess*?" Aladdin gasped.

Rasoul was surprised too, but he kept hold of Aladdin's arm. "My orders come from Jafar," he said, and he dragged Aladdin off to the dungeon.

Aladdin wondered what would become of him. He knew that no one had ever escaped from the palace dungeon.

A hunchbacked old man hobbled towards him. "I know a way out," he said.

Aladdin stared at him.

"I know the way to a cave filled with magnificent treasures," the old man went on. "One of them is a magic lamp. I'm too old and frail to get it myself, but if you help me get the lamp, I'll reward you with a share of the treasure."

Aladdin thought of Princess Jasmine. Maybe wealth would impress her. He certainly had no hope of winning her without it. "All right," he said to the old man. "Let's go."

The old man was really Jafar, in a clever disguise. He took Aladdin through a secret passage out to the desert. As they stood before the Cave of Wonders, Jafar held up his scarab medallion. The cave opened, and Aladdin stepped forward. Abu was right behind him.

"*Touch nothing but the lamp!*" boomed the voice of the Tiger-God as they went inside.

As Aladdin and Abu made their way through the cave, they gazed around in amazement. They could never have imagined such riches. There were mountains of coins, piles of gold, heaps of glittering jewels, bowls, goblets, treasures of every description.

But there was no sign of a magic lamp, and they hadn't a clue how to find it.

Suddenly Abu saw something move behind a mound of coins. Aladdin went to take a closer look, and found a carpet – a moving carpet! It seemed to be pointing towards something.

"It must be a magic carpet!" exclaimed Aladdin. "Let's follow it, Abu!"

The carpet led them to a deep cavern with a tall tower of rock in the centre. On top of the tower, lit by a magical light, stood the lamp.

Aladdin got ready to climb the tower. "Wait here," he told Abu. "And remember, don't touch *anything*."

But Abu had spotted a magnificent jewel in the hands of a monkey-god, and he couldn't resist it. Just as Aladdin reached for the lamp, Abu grabbed the jewel.

Suddenly, with a terrible rumbling, the walls of the cave collapsed. The jewels and piles of treasure melted into pools of red-hot lava, and Aladdin tumbled towards his doom.

With an amazing burst of speed, the carpet rushed down and rescued Aladdin and Abu.

But there was no way out of the cave now. They were trapped. All they had was the lamp.

Aladdin held it up. "I wonder what's magic about this old thing," he said, rubbing off some of the dust.

Suddenly –
POOOOF!

Colourful smoke poured from the spout of the lamp, forming itself into a blue cloud. Slowly the cloud began to take shape – and became an enormous genie!

The Genie held his head and twisted his neck round. "Ten thousand years cooped up in that lamp will give you *such* a crick in the neck!" he exclaimed. "But it's nice to be back. Now, what can I do for you, Master?"

"*Master?*" said Aladdin. "I'm your master?"

"Yes," said the Genie, "and I can grant you three wishes. There are just a few limitations: I can't kill anyone, I can't make anyone fall in love with anyone else, and I can't bring anyone back from the dead."

Aladdin wasn't sure whether or not to believe in this Genie, so he decided to put him to the test.

"Whoever heard of a genie with limitations?" he said. "You're probably not a real genie at all. I'll bet you can't even get us out of this cave!"

"You don't believe me?" said the Genie, offended. He grabbed Aladdin and Abu and put them on the carpet. "Just sit down and we're out of here!"

With a great *WHOOOSH!* the carpet zoomed up and out of the cave. Aladdin was free!

"All right," said the Genie, as they came down in a desert oasis. "No more freebies. Now, what's your first wish?"

Once again, Aladdin thought of Princess Jasmine. The Genie couldn't make her fall in love with him, but perhaps... "I wish to become a prince!" he said.

The Genie waved his hand. Instantly Aladdin was dressed in a prince's cloak of the finest silk. On his head was a beautiful jewelled turban. Abu was turned into the regal elephant that would carry Aladdin into Agrabah.

Later that day, a magnificent procession made its way to the Sultan's palace. At the centre of the procession was Aladdin, now called Prince Ali Ababwa.

"I have journeyed from afar to seek your daughter's hand," he said, bowing to the Sultan.

The Sultan was very impressed. "I think you'll like this one," he told Jasmine.

He was wrong. Jasmine was still angry at the whole idea. "I refuse to have my future decided for me!" she said as she stormed out of the room.

Somehow, Aladdin had to change her mind. So that night he flew up to Jasmine's balcony on the magic carpet and invited her for a ride over the city.

As they swooped and soared across the moonlit sky, with stars twinkling all around them, Jasmine felt her heart soar as well. When they said good night, Jasmine looked into Prince Ali's eyes and knew that here, after all, was a prince she did want to marry. She had never been so happy!

There was one person, though, who was not at all happy – Jafar. This Prince Ali could get in the way of all his plans to take over the kingdom. He had to get rid of him!

When Aladdin left Princess Jasmine's balcony, he was stopped by Jafar's guards. Before he knew what was happening, he was bound and gagged. Looking around wildly, he saw that Abu had been tied up too. Even the carpet had been caught and thrown in a cage. Aladdin was a prisoner once more!

But this time he wasn't taken to the dungeon. Instead, a heavy ball was chained to his ankles and he was pushed off a cliff into the sea. He sank straight to the bottom.

Aladdin was drowning. The lamp, which had been hidden under his turban, began drifting away. Using the last of his strength, Aladdin stretched his hand out to touch it.

SPLOOSH! The Genie appeared. "Please make a wish!" he begged Aladdin. "I can't help you unless you tell me to. Say, *Genie, I want you to save my life!*"

Aladdin's head bobbed weakly.

"I'll take that as a yes!" exclaimed the Genie. The next moment, Aladdin was flying with the Genie back to Agrabah.

Aladdin got to the palace just in time. Jafar had hypnotised the Sultan with his serpent staff, and the Sultan was about to force Jasmine to marry Jafar.

Leaping in through the window, Aladdin grabbed the staff and smashed it on the floor. The spell was broken – but not before Jafar glimpsed the lamp in Aladdin's turban.

The Sultan ordered his guards to seize Jafar, but the wicked counsellor quickly made his escape. He pulled out a magic pellet from his robes and threw it on the floor. In a puff of smoke he and Iago were gone.

Back in his tower, Jafar was deep in thought. "Now we know who Prince Ali really is," he said to Iago. "More important, we know he has the lamp." Suddenly he grinned fiendishly. "And you, Iago, are going to steal it for me!"

At dawn the next morning, Iago flew into Prince Ali's room, grabbed the lamp and took it back to Jafar.

As soon as he had the lamp, Jafar made his first wish – to be Sultan. The Genie had no choice but to grant it.

Within seconds Jasmine's father was stripped of his Sultan's robes. Sadly, the Genie moved the entire palace to a mountain top outside the city.

Then Jafar made his second wish – to be the most powerful sorcerer in the world. He immediately turned Prince Ali back into Aladdin and banished him, Abu and the carpet to a far-off snowy wasteland. Now there was no one to stand in Jafar's way.

"Agrabah is mine!" the new Sultan cried triumphantly.

Weak and shivering with cold, Aladdin struggled to rescue Abu and the magic carpet from the drifting snow. There was no time to lose. They had to get back to Agrabah.

By the time they arrived, it was almost too late. Jafar had turned the Sultan into a puppet on a string and was getting ready to make Jasmine his queen. Jasmine tried desperately to escape – until she spied Aladdin at the window.

"Jafar," she said sweetly, to distract him, "I never noticed how incredibly handsome you are!"

As a smiling Jafar turned to hear more, Aladdin made his move.

But he didn't get very far. Jafar saw him reflected in Jasmine's crown and whirled round, furious.

"How many times do I have to kill you, boy?" he shrieked, striking Aladdin with his serpent staff.

Jafar turned back to Jasmine. "Deceiving shrew!" he snarled. "Your time is up!" He trapped her inside a giant hourglass filled with sand that could bury her alive. Then he sent a shower of swords down around Aladdin.

"You cowardly snake!" shouted Aladdin, coming towards Jafar with one of the swords.

"You'll see how snakelike I can be!" replied Jafar, holding up his staff.

Horrified, Aladdin watched as Jafar turned himself into a hideous, giant cobra surrounded by a deadly wall of fire. Roaring and hissing, the monster lunged towards Aladdin.

"Now," thundered Jafar, wrapping himself round Aladdin, "did you think you could outwit the most powerful being on earth?"

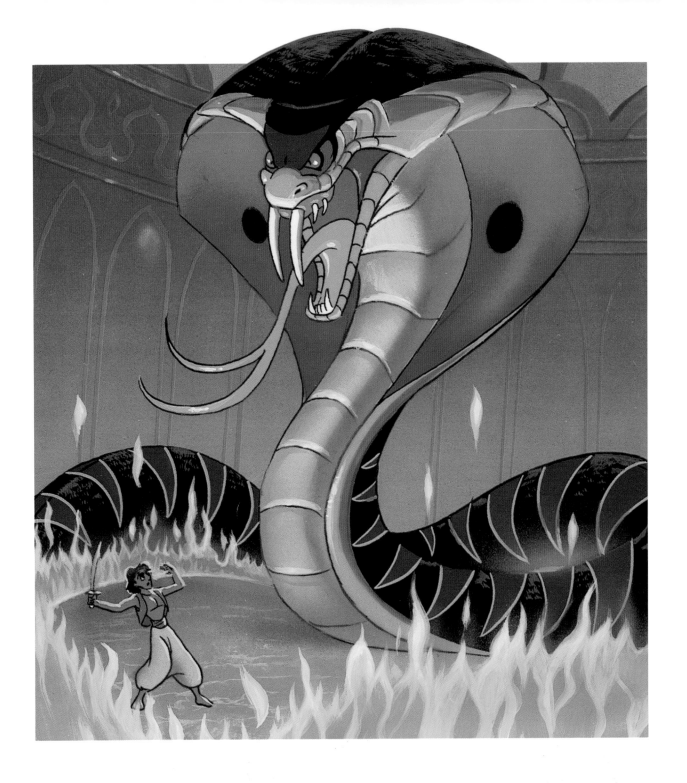

Aladdin thought quickly.

"You're not so powerful," he said to Jafar. "The Genie is much more powerful than you are. He gave you your power. He can take it away!"

Jafar knew this was right. He loosened his hold on Aladdin. "Slave!" he bellowed to the Genie. "This is my third wish! I wish to be – an all-powerful genie!"

All at once a current of energy surrounded Jafar. His shape began to change. "Yes!" he shrieked. "Absolute power!"

Then, suddenly, a lamp appeared beneath him. Aladdin grabbed it. "You wanted to be a genie!" he cried, holding the lamp out to Jafar. "You've got your wish – and everything that goes with it!"

"No!" screamed Jafar, terrified. "*NOOOOO!*" But he was unable to stop himself being sucked into the lamp's spout along with Iago.

"Aladdin, you little genius!" chuckled the Genie, when Jafar had disappeared. He took the lamp out to the balcony and flung it towards the desert. "Ten thousand years in the Cave of Wonders ought to chill him out!" he said.

Inside, the room had returned to normal. Jasmine's hourglass had disappeared, and the Sultan was his full size again, dressed in his royal robes. Smiling, the Genie picked up the palace and took it back to its rightful place in Agrabah.

"I'm sorry I lied to you," Aladdin said to Jasmine. "I'm not really a prince."

"But I still love you," said Jasmine. "I want to marry you! If it wasn't for that stupid law!"

"You still have one more wish," the Genie reminded Aladdin. "I can make you a prince again."

But Aladdin knew how the Genie yearned to be free. "No," he said. "I wish for your freedom." At once the Genie was released from his lamp.

Suddenly the Sultan stepped forward. "We need a new law," he said. "The Princess may now marry anyone she chooses!" And of course, she chose Aladdin.

As the Genie flew off to his new life, Jasmine and Aladdin shared a kiss. There was a new life ahead of them too – a life filled with happiness.